Ingrid & Dieter Schubert

Hammer Soup

Kate kept a tidy house and a weeded garden and she never shared her vegetables with anyone!

One morning a *bang! bang! bang!* woke her up, and when she leaned out her window what did she see...

…but a giant! Next door! Building a monstrosity!

The giant, Bruce, smiled and invited Kate for dandelion tea.

"Ugh, dandelions!" Kate said. "Nasty weeds."

Soon she was fencing in her garden, all the way around.

All summer, Kate worked and Bruce played.
   Whenever he invited Kate to go fishing, she
was too busy doing chores.
   "You should do something useful," she said.
   "Oh, maybe tomorrow," he answered.

And sometimes there was a surprise
waiting for Kate outside her door.

In the fall, Kate gathered apples for the
winter. "You should, too," she told Bruce.
   Bruce said, "Maybe tomorrow." Birds
whistled in the weeds of his garden.

In the winter, Kate's house was warm and cozy; Bruce's was cold and drafty. *It is his own fault,* Kate thought. *I warned him.*

In his house, Bruce shivered and told himself, *I'll fix it tomorrow. Things could be worse.*

That night, a raging storm shook the shack until it creaked and groaned, and finally a gust of wind blew Bruce's house into the air.

"This is terrible," Kate cried.

"It could be worse," Bruce answered, through chattering teeth.

Kate brought Bruce into her house. What else could she do?

"But you can't eat up my food," she told him.

"Of course not," Bruce said. "But if you have a pan with water and a bit of salt, I could make us some delicious hammer soup."

"Hammer soup?" Kate said. Her tummy was rumbling.

She put a pan of water on the stove and added salt.
Carefully Bruce lowered his hammer into the pan.
They took turns stirring, but when Kate tasted it
she said, "Yuck! It's bland!"

"Well," Bruce said, "it needs some nails, but
maybe a sausage would do."

"Good idea," Kate said.

She added the sausage and tasted again. "Too thin," she decided.

"Too bad I didn't bring any bolts," said Bruce. "Maybe some chopped carrots would do?"

Kate rushed to the cellar and returned with an armload: carrots, potatoes, beans, and a pumpkin. The two cooks sliced the vegetables and put them in the pan.

The finished soup was so scrumptious they ate it all— every bit but the hammer!

"Imagine all the terrific things you could make with this hammer!" Kate said.

Bruce thought of his house, stuck high in a tree.

"I could fix my house with it," he said with a sigh.

"Yes," Kate said. "There's plenty to do. But it will wait until tomorrow."